LOST GIRL

Who Am I?

LOST GIRL
Who Am I?

D. Caldwell

Published by ***Caldwell***
DLC2

Published by Caldwell DLC2

Library of Congress Cataloging-in-Publication Data
Caldwell, D.
Lost Girl: Who Am I?
D. Caldwell

ISBN: 978-0-578-41421-8

Dedication

I dedicate this book to my husband Eddie Caldwell and my daughter Jordin Caldwell. They are my biggest supporters.

Contents

Acknowledgments

First, I give thanks to my sister, Venay Savoy, and my dear friend Gilda Squire. I expressed an interest in writing a few years ago. Neither of them turned me away; instead what they did was offer advice and guide me in the right direction. I was not an avid reader, so Venay and Gilda were my literary muses and introduced me to a wide genre of books. My appreciation of the art of writing was nourished, and I soon realized I too was a storyteller and wanted to become a writer. It took years to reach this level of understanding, but today I love to read and write thanks to these two ladies.

Equally important was how when I was growing up my mother pushed me to partake in a variety of puzzles and word games. I was reluctant to do so. My mother was adamant and told me this would help broaden my vocabulary skills and introduce me to many new words. She was absolutely correct.

Lastly, I acknowledge my daughter Jordin Caldwell, who is a great influence on my life. She is a creative spirit and has helped pull out the creative side of me that once laid dormant. As a mother, I look up to her and love the passion and fuel she pours into any challenge she faces.

Introduction

A journey is a “passage or progress from one state to another.” Emily feels as though she is lost and is in search of truth and revelations. Being lost is “unable to find one’s way; not knowing one’s whereabouts.” With all of this, how does Emily know what path to take? Will Emily let her life-decisions and emotions drive her in the direction she needs to go, or will she listen to reason?

Confiding in others is not easy to do, as she holds everything inside. What will be the key to opening Emily’s treasure chest, and to revealing new and old secrets? Is Emily strong enough to take that personal journey? Will she break at the challenge or will she push through? Emily has the key, but it’s buried deep within. Will she let someone help to unlock her secrets? Finding the answer is the treasure of this story.

ONE: *WHO AM I?*

I'm Emily Sims, the daughter of Branford Sims and Eloise Sims. Everyone called mamma "Lizzy," a name she preferred over Eloise. I grew up in a small town in South Carolina named Lexington. I was popular throughout my school years—at Lexington High School I was elected the president of the Student Council and Homecoming queen in my junior and senior years.

People used to always say I had a presence when I walked into a room. I am a petite young woman with caramel-colored skin and hazel eyes. A lot of people say I'm beautiful—a beautiful, young black female. My hair is silky black, and I normally wear it pulled back into flowing, cascading curls. While I was told I illuminated a natural beauty inside and out, this "beauty" also has brought me problems with men. By the time I was in high school, I would always wear hipster-style baggy jeans or overalls with a T-shirt. I wore something like this every day—you see, I was afraid to show off my figure or wear make-up because of the unwanted attention and how I was treated. Though I did start showing a promiscuous_side by my senior year. But that's for later…

Dating back to when I was a young girl, whenever I wore shorts or sundresses, I was approached with seductive and disgusting comments and stares—even by men in my own family. Yes, I've faced many obstacles in my life. I began to cover myself up all of the time, no matter how hot the temperature got in the summer. And South Carolina is known to have hot and humid summers.

My fears of men went unspoken; I didn't even feel comfortable confiding to my mother. So, she didn't understand why I always covered up my body or shrank into a shell whenever family came around. I held unto this secret for many years for fear of it destroying my family.

Even with all of this, I persevered. I remained deeply immersed in my studies. I graduated with honors and was accepted to many colleges while winning offers of scholarships and grants. My family was anxious to find out which school I would select. Finally, the day arrived when I would announce what my decision would be. Our regular family Sunday dinner would be the day.

I contemplated over and over again how I would break the news to the family, and more importantly, mamma. I asked mamma one day, "If I decide not to tell the family which college I chose, how would that make the family feel?"

Mamma replied, "I have always told you family is important and WE KEEP NO SECRETS!"

I thought to myself, true, but is it really true? I continued to wonder if breaking the news to the family over Sunday dinner was a good idea; then it hit me—what is wrong with me? This is how we always handled huge events and announcements in our family. We always discussed life changing events over dinner at mamma's and daddy's house. I looked in the mirror and told myself to stop being silly. I can do it. Indeed, who am I? I am Emily Sims, the daughter of Branford Sims and Eloise Sims.

TWO: *SUNDAY DINNER*

The aromas in the house on Sunday afternoons were always delightful. Mamma would prepare a sumptuous meal with two or three desserts to follow. This Sunday, mamma said she would cook my favorite dishes. This brought a smile to my face and a tickle in my tummy. Mamma made lump crab cakes, pan-fried red snapper with sautéed shrimp in a butter and garlic sauce, fresh green beans mixed with garden-fresh tomatoes and onions, jasmine rice, and a fresh, mixed-green salad. The salad had bright colorful vegetables picked from mamma's famous garden. For dessert, mamma made homemade vanilla ice cream that she topped with toasted pecans, drizzled with warm caramel and smothered with whipped cream; a strawberry shortcake dripping with strawberries, blueberries and raspberries; and she made a key-lime pie, too. I could hardly wait for everyone to arrive.

Dinner always started promptly at 5 p.m. By 3:45, everyone began showing up. We were soon seated around our huge, beautiful mahogany dining-room table, which comfortably sat twelve. Daddy, who carved out the table with his own hands, made it large enough for us to enjoy dinner as an extended family.

It took daddy four years to finish his gift. He worked on it in the basement of our home whenever he could find time from his regular job. To provide for the family, daddy had to put in really long hours as an airplane mechanic at Fort Jackson in Columbia, South Carolina. It was at Fort Jackson where daddy befriended a Mr. Henry Hutchkins. Mr. Hutchkins would come by the house on occasion to go fishing with daddy or they would go have a couple of beers at a local bar called Smokey's. Mamma and daddy would entertain a lot, but with childhood friends and family. Daddy was a stickler about not bringing work into his home and that included his co-workers, except Mr. Hutchkins—on occasion.

During daddy's creative downtime, I would be reminded of his love for music, often hearing what we today call "oldies but goodies"—music like the Temptations, the Four Tops, and James Brown blasting from his workroom. When I heard such sounds coming from the basement, particularly daddy's loud singing, I knew he was working on his masterpiece, his baby. There is so much detail in every inch of the design. All of our names are engraved in the legs of the table, but tastefully done as a work of art. It's absolutely beautiful. I know daddy smiles from heaven as he looks upon us every time the family sits at the table for dinner.

Hours before, while setting the table, I kept thinking of daddy. How he had died five years earlier after succumbing to his battle with cancer. Since then, every time we have Sunday dinner and I'm setting the table, I can't help but think of him and give praise. It was hard to believe that he was gone.

So, I kept thinking, how I missed daddy so much, especially when I had big moments like this, as I nervously considered how I would tell the family about my choice of a college. Daddy and I had been very close. I wished he were there, so I could turn to him to seek his advice and approval as I always had.

It was 5 p.m. and everyone was seated. On this day, mamma, as usual, sat at the head of the table, and I sat at the other end, per her request. Mamma told the family that it was a special day—that at the end of dinner, I was going to announce the college I had selected to attend. I would be the second in my family to go to college. My Aunt June was the first when she attended Spelman College, an African American all girl's school in Atlanta, so this was a big deal for everyone. Mamma then led the family in prayer to bless the food, and soon after we began piling our plates with the feast.

You could hear laughter around the table, forks clinging against the plates at every scoop, and glasses tapping the table after every sip. The food was *soooo* good. I was unbelievably delighted. How could I want to give this up every Sunday? I told myself, I will and there was no turning back. I can still come back to visit and have Sunday dinners too, right? As soon as thoughts of doubt creeped into my head, I quickly came to my senses. ...

When dinner was over, the table was cleared and prepared for dessert. By now, I was so nervous from what I was about to announce, I was trembling and perspiring heavily. I had no idea what the family would think, especially mamma. During dessert, Mamma spoke again to all around the table to quiet the chatter. She then said the floor was mine.

I just sat there nervously, and then smiled for a moment as I looked around the room. I slowly began to speak. Before I knew it, the words "Boston University" blurted from my lips. I stopped. There was dead silence.

It was as though the wind was knocked out of me. I couldn't speak or move. And mamma seemed stunned. I wanted to comfort her, but I sat there frozen in my thoughts.

Then mamma said, "Baby, where is that school located?"

Suddenly, I snapped out of my trance. I began to answer mamma as calmly as possible. I lowered my head and said, "Boston, mamma. Boston, Massachusetts. In the Northeast."

Mamma began weeping loudly and uncontrollably. She could not believe that she would be living in the family home alone. I began to hear mumbling from family members, comments such as "selfish," "good for her," "what's wrong with her," "congratulations," and "evil," and so on.

I got up from daddy's table and walked out of the room. I stepped outside to take a walk and to clear my head. No one understood why I made the decision I chose, or why I was, as someone said, "Leaving the family." And South Carolina. No one even asked. ...

As I walked to the park, these pesky thoughts kept creeping into my head. I finally made it there after walking a mile or so. I sat in the grass by the lake and started crying. How could good news turn out to be so bad, I thought? Then I felt a cool breeze sweep across me. While it was welcoming because of the scorching heat, it also was frightening. I shivered a little and then I began to smile. It was as though something or someone was comforting me. I began to pray. Then I started talking to daddy. I could hear him speak and remember him always saying, “Baby girl, don’t let anything or anyone defeat you or change your mind when you set goals.” That was when I felt sure that the cool breeze was daddy reaching out to me. I sat quietly for another thirty minutes before I walked home.

I began thinking how I couldn’t wait for August to get here so I could be on my way. I wanted to be on a journey to erase some of the pain from my past, including the insecurity caused by some of my male family members. I hoped it would be a new beginning.

THREE: *THE TALK*

I returned home after a two-hour reprieve from the announcement and walked into a quiet house. Everyone had left, leaving me to return to an empty space, silent and still, and reflect on my decision. I went to my room and sat on my bed and began to write in my journal. Soon I laid back and I turned on my radio, so I could listen to "Jazz in the Night," which played jazz music every evening from 8 p.m. to 10 p.m. One of my favorite things to do is listen to jazz when I am relaxing, studying or need to clear my head. Deep in my thoughts, I began to hear a smooth melody by Dee Dee Bridgewater playing—I always found her voice comforting…

I didn't realize that I had dozed off until I faintly heard a door close and a car leaving the driveway. Becoming alert, I guessed mamma must have returned. I heard slow footsteps climb the staircase and then a soft knock on my door. I answered by inviting mamma into my room. We sat on my bed and began talking.

“Mamma,” I said, “it’s time for me to leave and make it on my own. Academically and financially, it was the best choice for me. I have to set my path for my future and grow into an independent woman.” The more I talked the more it felt like I was also trying to convince myself.

“I understand, baby,” mamma said. “And I’ll support you and all of your decisions as long as they make sense. I will be here for you no matter what.”

I hugged mamma tightly and told her I loved her.

Mamma said that after my announcement, she had spoken with Aunt June and she was going to move in with mamma. I screamed with excitement. I was so happy for mamma; Aunt June is one of my favorite aunties.

FOUR: *MY CONFIDANT*

Aunt June is the most beautiful person, both spiritually and physically. She is a tall, statuesque goddess, with a golden honey complexion, gray eyes, and long, blonde curly locs. I adored her so much that I grew my hair out, so I could wear it just like hers. People often mistake me for her daughter because we look so much alike and have many of the same mannerisms.

Aunt June is a successful entrepreneur. She owns several South Carolina businesses, both in Columbia and Charleston. She has a home interior design business in Columbia and an eclectic art gallery in Charleston, and she is renowned for both her art and design style. Many celebrities, political officials, and businessmen and businesswomen fly Aunt June all over the world to engage her expertise.

It was when Aunt June was away for an extended period of time that I was traumatized and knocked off my feet with disbelief, hurt, and anger. When Aunt June returned, she instinctively knew something was different. We often would stay up all night and talk. I still did not reveal everything to Aunt June but confided in her about certain issues. We talked about love, sex, friendship, boys, men and dating. This time, Aunt June sensed that I was holding something back. She looked quizzically and said, “Sugar, are you okay?”

I only responded with a slight smile. Then she said there was sadness in my eyes. I held out and said nothing. Mamma could never detect my most inner emotions as Aunt June could. Mamma was much older and almost like a grandma, although a jazzy one. Aunt June and I were closer in age, like an older and younger sister. We were sixteen years apart. Still, the significance of our age difference never dawned on me. Nor the time she had spent living in our house when I was young. These were things I never thought about. Not once.

Even to find out later in life that mamma was not as naïve or clueless as I once thought was somewhat revealing. Mamma commented that she knew us better than we knew ourselves.

FIVE: *BEST FRIENDS*

Although I was close to Aunt June, I had a best friend named Seneca, who I confided in even more. Seneca was this voluptuous Latina firecracker—her mom is from Colombia and her dad, born in New York City, is black and of Jamaican descent. Seneca was five feet six inches tall, with curves for days. She was of an olive-colored complexion, with long, black wavy hair showcasing blonde highlights. Her eyes were coal black, and her strikingly beautiful face featured the cutest dimples and a small black beauty mark above her lips. She has an infectious smile and distinctly bubbly laugh. One look at Seneca and you just knew she was a sex kitten down for whatever.

We had so much fun together. I was the shy girl and she was the life of the party. No one knew of the lengths we'd go to have a good time. I would call Seneca and say, "Let's do something!" Seneca would always respond, "You ain't said nothing but a word. I am on my way, so be ready!" But I had to portray a clean image while Seneca was herself at all times. I admired that about her. We'd look each other up and down, burst out laughing, and say, "Let's do this thing called 'Life!'" The SHIT was always popping when we got together. We loved to party in Savannah and Augusta, Georgia. We only went to Atlanta, Georgia, on weekend rendezvous with our men, as the lively neighboring state to South Carolina, Georgia became our home away from home. No one we knew would ever see us do our dirt, turn up or act a fool in Augusta, Savannah or Atlanta. Yes Lord, the turn up was real, as was the partying and the guys. We always had fun and never had to pay a dime. That's how we knew we were bad to the bone and sexy as hell—even with my clean image. I knew how to draw them in with my seductive eyes and the sway of hips as I sashayed when I walked.

Around that time, I started turning my attention to my English teacher, Mr. Jonathan Saxton. He was *sooo* fine and I had a crush on him. It was hard for me to concentrate when I was around him. He had a muscular build, piercing eyes, and his lips looked soft and subtle. He reminded me of the actor, Omari Hardwick. Mr. Saxton was also twelve years my senior, but I didn't care.

I often daydreamed of the things I wanted him to do to me. In class, I would have visions of Mr. Saxton laying me down on his desk and sensually licking me from head to toe. Every time I left his class, I was sweating and pulsating everywhere. I knew then I had to satisfy my urge and my sexual craving for him, one way or another. Outwardly shy and reserved, I have another side: I always go for what I want, by any means necessary. I said to myself over and over again, "I will have Mr. Saxton. OH YES I WILL!"

One day I decided that I would make my move. I stayed after school for a tutoring session with Mr. Saxton. I walked up to his desk to ask him a question and then as I walked past him to go back to my seat, I gazed into his eyes and rubbed up against him.
He looked at me and shook his head disapprovingly.

The seed had been planted. After that day, I would catch him making quick glances toward me. I would respond with a sly and mischievous smirk. I never saw a wedding ring or pictures of a family, so I figured, even though he was much older than me, he was fair game. I had already turned 18 and felt like I was a grown woman. I had lost my virginity to an old boyfriend when I was 16. Now I was ready to experience lovemaking with a sexy, grown man.

One day after school Seneca and I went to Columbia Mall to grab some dinner. Seneca's parents had bought her a Honda Accord as an early graduation present. I began to tell her about Mr. Saxton and how I wanted him—badly. Seneca told me to be careful, but to continue giving him subtle signals of my interest in him. Then Seneca began to tell me that she met a man, this guy named Keith, who lived in a small town named Sumpter.

"Interesting," I told her. "I have a cousin named Keith who lives in Sumpter. He is married with two kids."

Seneca shook her head, and said, "No, this can't be the same Keith. My Keith has never discussed a wife or kids."

"If he was cheating on his wife, do you think he would tell you any of that?" I asked.

Seneca continued to describe Keith, and then I knew it. Her Keith was indeed my cousin. We both looked at each other and were like, OH Shit!!!

Seneca and Keith had been seeing each other for about three months. Meanwhile, Mr. Saxton and I finally hooked up about a month after I spoke with Seneca about him. The four of us would go on dates in Augusta, Georgia, and book hotel rooms for fear of anyone seeing us. The sex with Mr. Saxton was explosive. He had my head spinning and I felt like I was falling in love. He taught me how to explore my body and his orally, and through more traditional sex. Damn the sex was great! We almost always used condoms, but we slipped up a few times because it felt even better in the raw. On those occasions when we didn't use condoms, Mr. Saxton would use the pullout method.

We decided to go away for the weekend with Seneca and Keith, and this time we rented a two-bedroom condo in Savannah, Georgia. That first night, we all were drinking, and smoking weed, and it got hot and heavy real fast. We all started ripping off our clothes and began having sex in the family room in front of each other. It didn't bother any of us; in fact, it turned us on even more hearing each other in ecstasy. Then it happened, Mr. Saxton and I came to together. It was so invigorating. We lay there sweating and panting in each other's arms, not considering what we had done.

Needless to say, a month later I found out I was pregnant. I told Mr. Saxton and he went ballistic.

"There is no way you are keeping that baby. I am married with kids!" he screamed.

I looked at him with confusion, brokenhearted and distraught. I couldn't believe what I was hearing. Did he just say he was married with a family? I slapped the shit out of him and ran as far away from him as I could. It was the end of the school year, and I didn't want to see him anymore.

I was a complete basket-case. I cried all the time. I would sob with my head buried in my pillows, so mamma wouldn't hear me. I would cry in the bathroom with the water running. All the make- up I wore and ice packs I used to lessen the puffiness around my swollen eyes was becoming just too much to continue. I had to lie and tell mamma I was suffering from allergies. And she bought that lie, too, or so I thought. Then one day I called Seneca and asked if I could stay the night with her. Seneca said, “No need to ask, I am here for you.” I loved Seneca; she was and had always been my rock. I always kept clothes at her house, so I called mamma and told her I was staying at Seneca’s. Mamma said, “Okay, baby.” I felt sure then that mamma didn’t detect anything regarding my physical condition.

Keith and Seneca took me to an abortion clinic that next day. This was the start of my hiding behind a wall and covering up my body again. My fears of someone taking advantage of me had resurfaced in a big way. I was concerned that one day another man would not be truthful, just as Mr. Saxton had not been.

I also grew more concerned for Seneca. I told her she and Keith had to break up, but she ignored my pleas. Eventually, Seneca and I drifted apart. This was especially true once her relationship with Keith finally came to an end. She even believed I hurt their relationship by bringing them bad karma. We kept in touch, but didn't hang out as much. We were both hurt, but learned a valuable lesson: men will lie to you to get what they want, especially if they're married with children.

SIX: *THE UNTOLD TRUTH*

It was two months before college classes were to start and I needed to get my registration documents together. The university required personal and family financial information and vital papers, including my birth certificate, for the completion of my enrollment and for my scholarship. I told mamma I needed my birth certificate, so I could get a passport because I planned to participate in the student exchange program and travel overseas.

Mamma sighed and said that she knew this day would come, and she handed me a Bible and a diary. I wondered why she was doing this, giving me a Bible, and why she seemed so melancholy. I was instructed not to read the diary until later that evening. I thought that was an odd request and who did this mysterious diary belong to?

"Baby, you have to keep prayer and the Lord close to your heart," Mamma said.

"Okay," I answered, becoming concerned about what seemed to be mamma's mounting sorrow.

"There are two envelopes in the Bible for you," mamma said, slowly, and softly, almost whispering. "Open each envelope and call me if you need me."

Again, I said, "Okay."

I was confused by this whole exchange. I sat on my bed and flipped through the pages of the Bible until I came across the first envelope. I opened it and there was a check for $15,000. There also was a letter from daddy stating that this money was for school. I was elated. I had only saved $5,000 from my part-time job. The letter went on to explain additional monies had been placed in a trust fund, accessible once I graduated college.

Then I opened the second envelope. There was another letter from daddy, papers that said "adoption," and a birth certificate. I began to read daddy's letter and it wasn't long before I was crying uncontrollably. Apparently, daddy had had an affair off and on for years with a Mrs. Judith Hutchkins. Daddy and Mrs. Hutchkins had met when he was in the military, and they had begun the relationship while daddy was on tour in Germany. At the time, daddy and mamma were newlyweds, but after months of trying to have a baby they found that mamma couldn't have kids. This caused both of them considerable pain. Both were deeply affected and daddy and momma handled their grief in solitary ways. Momma became closed off, isolated to a degree. She had had one of her long-term dreams ripped away. Daddy also, was torn apart. He too had always wanted to have a family and had planned on building enough wealth to leave for mamma and his children to live comfortably when he died. Daddy confided in Mrs. Hutchkins and this was the start of an intimate bond.

It wasn't long before Mrs. Hutchkins became pregnant. Initially, she was hesitant to tell daddy—she knew he was married. But the time finally came when she had to reveal her secret. Mrs. Hutchkins was surprised to hear daddy say he wanted to keep that bundle of joy that was growing inside of her.

Mrs. Hutchkins cried tears of joy but knew there was no way she could raise the child. Although she had fallen deeply in love with daddy, Mrs. Hutchkins knew he only lusted for her. Mamma was the woman he always loved. Mrs. Hutchkins and daddy both knew sexually it was magical for them, but their relationship could go no further than that.

When the baby was born, mamma cried every night for weeks because she knew a child was something she couldn't give daddy. Eventually, after meeting Mrs. Hutchkins and being around the baby, mamma accepted and adopted the little one and raised her as her own. In reading daddy's letter, I learned that child is Aunt June. Not long after, they moved into a quiet tree-lined neighborhood of single-family houses. Mamma loved her new home and enjoyed raising Baby June in this environment.

There was so much more to learn. Daddy wrote that one day, the doorbell rang and mamma almost fainted when she saw Mrs. Hutchkins standing on her doorstep with a handsome man by her side. Mamma invited them in. Daddy almost choked on a beer when they walked in the Sims' home. Well, Mrs. Hutchkins and her newlywed husband, Mr. Henry Hutchkins, daddy's Fort Jackson coworker, had moved on their block. Everyone exchanged pleasantries and talked briefly. Mrs. Hutchkins never asked about the baby. Mamma could clearly see how much Aunt June was beginning to look like Mrs. Hutchkins, sharing her beautiful complexion, eyes and hair. Apparently, Mrs. Hutchkins never told her husband about the affair or the baby and the adoption…

Daddy had been oblivious to the fact that Mr. Hutchkins was in a serious relationship, planning a wedding, looking for a house, and not to mention, that he was preparing to marry daddy's concubine. When daddy got a chance to spend a minute alone with Mrs. Hutchkins, he pulled her in close to him, by touching her forearm and asked, "Do you know that I and Henry, your new husband, are friends? Did he ever mention my name?"

Mrs. Hutchkins said no, as she abruptly pulled away from daddy with tears starting to fall. Daddy felt guilty that he made her cry. Daddy hated to see women cry. He truly believed her, but this was such a weird and odd coincidence.

I had to stop reading to pull myself together. This was unbelievable. How could mamma have kept this a secret for all of these years? And I began wondering if Aunt June knew. I continued to read on…

Soon I found that daddy and Mrs. Hutchkins hooked up again, some 15 years after their original affair. I could not believe this had happened all over again. Mr. Hutchkins got so damn mad that he left home and moved up north for a year. In that time, Mrs. Hutchkins became pregnant. That's when I was born, he wrote…

I dropped the letter and screamed, "Holy Shit! What the hell is going on?" This is why Aunt June and I look so much alike and have a bond like no other, I thought. Mamma decided to raise me as her own, as she had done with Aunt June. Daddy vowed that he would never have an affair again and that he would remain faithful until his dying day.

Mamma forgave daddy, again, but told him that that woman should not be granted the right to keep the baby. She wanted to adopt me just as she had Aunt June. Daddy made sure mamma got her wish. This was the tawdry story of my damn life, and the secret that I was told the rest of the family had no knowledge of. That is except for Aunt June—mamma said she gave Aunt June a Bible that day as well, as Aunt June had not known the truth either.

I heard a knock on the door, and loud, persistent crying. It was Aunt June. We hugged each other tightly and sobbed for twenty minutes. Mamma soon came in. We were preparing to leave for a while, but she asked us before we left the house, to take the diary with us. We both turned around with tears in our eyes and anger in our hearts. We both asked something like, "Who gives a damn about an old worn-out diary after the shit we just learned?!"

Mamma spoke in a loud and stern voice, shouting "STOP JUST ONE MINUTE!" We both froze in our footsteps, looked at each other as to what the hell was going on—she had never spoken to us like that. Where did that voice come from? Mamma told us, "The only thing I have asked of your girls is to show me some respect. And damn it, regardless of what you just found out, you will respect me and this damn house!"

"Okay mamma," we said, "you are absolutely right, and we sincerely apologize for our response." Mamma responded, "Now take this box of Kleenex, wipe your faces and here is the worn-out old diary that I want you to read together."

We hesitantly took it and walked out of the front door confused as ever. We talked for hours and went on a walk by the lake. We agreed that mamma was to be forgiven, that it was unimaginable the hurt she had suffered over all of this time. We vowed we would keep this secret for as long as mamma wanted. This is one of many truths I hold close and dear to my heart, even all of these years later.

Aunt June gently took the diary from my hand and opened it slowly. The first page read, "The Diary of Lizzy." I delicately took the diary back from Aunt June, and began to read it aloud…

Daddy knew the time had come for him to reveal the truth to mamma. Daddy decided to take mamma on a dinner date to break the news and soften the blow by appeasing mamma with one of her wishes. Daddy told mamma that he needed to discuss a very important matter with her. He asked mamma to get dressed because he had made reservations at the small hideaway restaurant named LaRue, which is located in a secluded area of town. Mamma had always begged daddy to take her to this restaurant. They had a live jazz band there, served low-country seafood and soul food. This restaurant has always received rave reviews from the community's elites.

Mamma put on daddy's favorite dress. It was a crimson red and black wrap dress that stopped just above the knee. Mamma put on a pair of black five-inch stilettos. Her hair was pulled up into a bun, and she wore a dainty gold necklace with a two-karat single pear-shaped diamond charm and two-karat pear-shaped diamond earrings. Daddy was stunned at how gorgeous mamma looked. Mamma always wore palazzo-style pants and a short-sleeved cotton top or a maxi dress. But when mamma went out on the town, she always had heads turning. She was a lovely woman with elegant taste.

Daddy wore a simple Italian-cut suit, with a white crisp dress shirt, a black and gray hounds-tooth print tie and a handkerchief pocket square tucked neatly in his suit jacket's pocket. They both were equally pleased how one another looked. Mamma kept a picture of daddy of that night, tucked away in her jewelry box. Boy, I wished I was there to see this, I thought to myself, as I continued reading mamma's diary. Although I was hurt and angry, I could not wait to get to the next page. This letter gave me a new insight into mamma's gentle personality. I continue...

Daddy hoped that mamma would forgive him. This was the hardest thing daddy ever had to face in his life, he wrote. Daddy thought, "How do you tell the love of your life that you deceived them, broke their trust, lied and cheated to get what you always dreamed of having with them?" This night had to be special, from his heart and full of love. Daddy cried to himself: "My dear wife, how will she ever forgive me?" Daddy managed to pull himself together and took mamma out on the town. Daddy thought to himself this would be a night they would remember but may choose to forget. Daddy and mamma pulled up to the restaurant in daddy's all-white Cadillac. When they entered the restaurant, momma's and daddy's mouths dropped. It was beyond their expectations.

LaRue's had dim mood lighting, large mahogany wood tables and sleek chairs with plush mauve colored cushions. Beautiful votive candles flickered against the massive silver-framed mirrors that were adorned with the reflection of beautiful scented fresh flowers in huge chrome vases. The design was a mix of modern and southern styles. The hosts and waiters were adorned in black vests, white long sleeve shirts, white gloves with black slacks and shoes. Such elegance when you entered. The food was brought out on silver platters and served on white china.

Daddy arranged for them to sit in the balcony, which is normally reserved for VIP seating. Daddy had connections with the owners. Mamma was in such awe when she entered, she totally forgot why they were going there.

"Branford, how on earth did you pull this off?" Mamma said.

Daddy said, "Lizzy I am just as stunned as you!"

Daddy began telling mamma he met James and Natasha LaRue years ago at a small coffee shop when he was on tour in Germany. It was an instant connection. James served in the United States Marines for five years prior to meeting daddy. James and Natasha had a chance meeting while James was stationed in Germany and they fell instantly in love. Daddy and James stayed in contact over the years. James and Natasha talked about opening this restaurant and what they envisioned the restaurant to be. James told me once the restaurant was open, the invitation was extended to me with all the first-class perks. James and Natasha both came from wealthy families but were very humble. James and Natasha also knew of daddy's affair with Mrs. Hutchkins, but respected daddy's privacy. The opportunity to finally meet mamma was so exciting to Natasha. Secretly, Natasha held a special place for mamma in her heart, because she knew it would be devastating for anyone to find out about their spouse's infidelity.

After reading mamma's diary, I was puzzled about the story she told through Daddy's words, and I desperately wanted to see the picture of their night out, and for her to provide greater clarity. Aunt June and I returned home feeling drained, but open-minded for the conversation with mamma that we knew was about to happen. As soon as we returned home, we quietly retreated to my bedroom waiting for mama to join us. We hoped mamma could clear up some things and that our emotional state would not consume the conversation. Aunt June and I sat on my bed, each of us gripping a pillow and rocking back and forth in a somber state while anticipating mamma's gentle knock on the door.

Soon enough, Mamma knocked softly before entering the bedroom and sitting with me and Aunt June. It didn't take long for her to start again. She told us Daddy confessed to everything and provided every dirty little detail of the affair. That's when mamma reminded us that she had said to flip, carefully, through every page. That was when we found the picture clipped to a blank page in the diary near the back of the book. Aunt June and I were stunned at how beautiful mamma looked and how handsome Daddy was. Looking at this picture, no one would have ever thought our parents were on the very edge of divorce and suffering through the repercussions of an affair, and its accompanying lies and deceit.

PART 2

SEVEN: *THE MOVE*

My head was in a web of confusion and my heart was heavy. But it was time to go off on my new journey. That next morning, I rose up early to birds chirping, accompanied by a warm summer breeze blowing through my window and a beautiful sunrise. While it was very early in the morning, I could smell the aroma of breakfast in the air. I ran downstairs to find mamma with Aunt June, sitting at the kitchen table drinking coffee and reading the newspaper.

Mamma said, "Good morning, chile."

I smiled when I saw fresh fruit, her famous homemade French toast, and large chilled glasses of lime and cucumber water. I ran to hug mamma and Aunt June. There was sadness in the air, and silence, dead silence. The only thing you could hear was Aunt June flipping pages in the newspaper and mamma sipping her coffee.

As I continued to devour my food, suddenly I let out a loud belch. Mamma said, “Chile, you can’t stuff your face and eat that fast.

Aunt June added, “Exactly,” while laughing at me and shaking her head. “If you keep eating like that, you’re going to run all the boys away and maybe your future husband.”

“Well good,” Mamma said. “She only needs to concentrate on her studies and she can date after she graduates.”

I looked at both of them and said, “Really?” Then we all started laughing.

Mamma said, “Chile, go on upstairs and get ready.” I finished my breakfast and hurriedly ran upstairs to get my things together before my ride arrived.

I took a soothing shower, used my aromatherapy lotion and African body oil. I threw on some ripped jeans, a white T-shirt with my denim shirt tied around my waist, and a pair of pink Converse tennis shoes. Then I started grabbing my things, looking like a madwoman as I backed toward the door, pulling a couple of storage containers. Sweat was pouring down my face as if I were in a heavy rain. I was startled by giggles. Mamma and Aunt June were standing outside my door shaking their heads. They said in unison, "Girl, are you ever planning to return home to visit us?"

I stopped, looked at my things, and began laughing too. Finally, the atmosphere was light, and laughter was in the air at my expense. Still giggling, we hugged each other, as though there was forgiveness being released. Our spirits touched, and calmness wrapped its huge arms around us. The negative energy and feelings from the night before escaped us and we released one another and looked in each other's eyes. We all simply said, "I love you."

Mamma and Aunt June helped with the rest of my stuff. I quickly freshened up and changed my T-shirt. We waited on the front porch for my ride. More than two hours passed, but no one showed up. I began to cry, until I saw a black Chevy Tahoe pull up. Uncle Jimmy jumped out and shouted, "Surprise, baby girl!"

"What's going on?" I said, looking to Mamma and Aunt June.

Lo and behold, they walked back in the house and returned with their purses, jackets, and overnight bags. In tandem they said, "You know we weren't going to let our baby go off with strangers!"

Smiling from ear to ear, I began jumping up and down. Uncle Jimmy loaded the truck and we were off to Boston. Uncle Jimmy, who is mamma's only brother, is the nicest man I've ever known…

It was sixteen hours later when we finally arrived. We had made several rest stops for food and fuel. That evening we stayed at the Hyatt Regency Cambridge to get a good night's sleep and started fresh in the morning. The hotel was nice, but the view was even better. It was a wonderful reprieve from the long ride. Still, I laid in bed restless. I couldn't wait to see my dorm and I kept thinking about who my roommate would be, hoping she was nice and that we would get along. Finally, I dozed off.

When I awoke, it felt like I had slept for hours. I didn't realize at first that I had only gone to sleep at 5:00 a.m. and had only slept for two hours.

Everyone woke up early, and excitedly got ready for the day. We headed to the university, which was only two miles away. When we arrived, my eyes revealed a look of amazement. The fear in my heart was less evident. Although I was growing more and more frightened, I maintained my composure so my family wouldn't worry. My new life was getting ready to begin.

EIGHT: *COLLEGE LIFE*

It was later that evening and I was alone in my dorm. While I unpacked my things, Mamma and Aunt June had decorated my side of the dorm room. Not long after, Mamma, Aunt June and Uncle Jimmy were back on the highway.

It now was time for me to begin facing my fears, to grow up and be honest with myself. I had so many hidden secrets I hoped they wouldn't interfere with my studies. I laid on my bed and stared at the ceiling before drifting off to sleep.

I awoke to a loud knock at the door. I was startled; my roommate wasn't scheduled to move in until the next day. I jumped up and ran to answer the door. It was two girls I hadn't yet met. They asked if I wanted to go get pizza. Initially, I hesitated, and then thought what harm could it be? Maybe we would become friends.

It wasn't long before I learned otherwise. These two girls weren't interested in being my friend, they just wanted to party and drink. Since I'm not much of a drinker, needless to say that didn't work out too well. The situation with them was so uncomfortable that over the next few weeks it caused me to put up a protective barrier when meeting new people. My roommate and I, however, became instant friends. We had a lot of the same classes, our interests were similar, but our views differed when it came to dating.

My roommate's name was Sarah. She was a complicated, but intriguing individual. Sarah was all natural, and a free spirit, who loved people. She had brown skin, large black eyes, long eyelashes, and wore a short sassy haircut with no chemicals in her hair. She loved to wear vintage clothing that showed off her hourglass-shaped body.

One day that semester, Sarah told me she believed love or lovemaking was not limited to sharing with one gender, and that sexually, she experimented with both women and men. She said that she could show me intimacy and satisfaction that a man couldn't provide. I looked at

Sarah with confusion. I'd always seen her with men, never a woman. But Sarah said a woman has to completely know her body before she could fully satisfy any man—woman-to-woman intimacy could teach that. I was surprised and mystified. I began considering having a one-time experience with Sarah. But this first talk was not the time.

Instead, throughout the year, we continued to discuss sexuality and sexual preferences. These talks would go on for hours. Most times, we agreed that we had to complete our evening studies before we'd continue our heart-to-heart sessions.

One night, I came out the shower with my towel wrapped around my body and my hair pulled up—I had forgotten to take my robe in the bathroom. Sarah was sitting on her bed only wearing a T-shirt. I froze in my steps—before I had gone into shower, I thought she was asleep. I was wrong. Sarah got up and walked toward me seductively. She pushed my hair from my face. Some of my curls began to drop. Then she kissed me, on the lips. I pushed her away. She began to move away, but I found myself grabbing her by the arm. I pulled her back toward me. Sarah held me, and we kissed—first softly, then intensely, passionately, and with so much intimacy I lost myself. I didn't realize my towel had fallen to the floor…

To this day, Sarah is the best lover I have ever experienced, other than my husband. I hold a special place in my heart for her, and for our secret love affair. It went on for two years.

NINE: *FULL CIRCLE*

It has been five years since I graduated from Boston University. I had received my Bachelor of Arts degree in graphic design and media arts, and later, while pregnant with my second child, I earned my Master's in graphic design. I own a company named Graphic Design Limited that provides web design and digital art services to small businesses and corporate clients. I relocated to the West Coast, to sunny Sacramento, California, where I live with my husband—Mr. Jonathan Saxton. Yes, you heard me right. Let me tell you how Jonathan and I found each other again and ended up married with children.

During my senior year in college, I began having anxiety attacks and headaches—it was from built up stress. My dear friend Sarah was studying psychology and advised me to make an appointment with a psychologist. Eventually, I agreed, even though I was insecure about revealing my innermost secrets. I was graduating soon, and I increasingly grew nervous about what the future would bring. I was nearing the end of my college days and it was beginning to weigh heavily on me.

One Sunday evening during one of our heart-to-heart talks, Sarah gave me the business card of a Dr. Melinda Lawson. I reluctantly took the card. I called Dr. Lawson's office the next morning to make an appointment and grew nervous when I was told there was an opening the very next day. Throughout that day and into the night, there was a nagging feeling that wouldn't go away—I kept contemplating why I shouldn't go to the appointment. I awoke Tuesday morning at 4:00 a.m. to prepare myself for what I assumed would be a very intrusive experience, one that could be life changing.

Let me be clear: I was totally against seeing a therapist. I always thought my friends and family, and members of my church were the best people to speak with. As I prepared that morning, I shook those thoughts out of my head, took a hot shower, got dressed and headed to my 9:00 a.m. appointment. When I arrived a lovely girl at the receptions desk greeted me. She gave me tons of paperwork to fill out before the consultation. I read the confidentiality statement on the consent form and felt relieved that my innermost thoughts would not be exposed to anyone without my permission. I turned in the paperwork and sat patiently in the waiting room. It was quite calming—the walls were a soft gray with white frosted light fixtures that illuminated a soft glow. There were beautiful flowing digital waterfalls, and peaceful paintings of God's finest natural scenes.

"Emily Sims, we are ready for you," a soothing voice suddenly snapped me out of my tranquility.

I got up and walked slowly to Dr. Lawson's office.

A petite woman, who displayed a strong presence, greeted me with a firm, but subtle handshake. Dr. Lawson wore a red, sassy short haircut that was spiked in the front and tapered on the sides. Her face was sprinkled with small freckles on smooth vanilla skin and highlighted by deep sky-blue eyes. She wore a light-gray pants suit, a pink and white floral print blouse, and a pair of gray platform shoes with four-inch heels.

With the way she carried herself, she looked exquisite.

She welcomed me into her office, which had a large mahogany and maple desk that sat across from a deep cranberry-colored leather sofa and chairs. Dr. Lawson asked that I sit on the sofa and she sat facing me in one of the chairs—this was more welcoming than her sitting behind the desk. We then went through a few basic questions.

Dr. Lawson began by asking, “So Emily, tell me what brought you here today?” She added, “I hope you don’t mind me calling you Emily. I want your visit to be informal and provide a comforting space for you.”

I responded in a soft monotone voice, telling her calling me Emily was okay. Dr. Lawson spoke again to get my attention by saying, “Emily, you seem a little nervous and you keep twirling your hair through your fingers.”

I sat there in a stupor looking out the window.

Dr. Lawson spoke again trying to get me to snap out of it. “Well. let me tell you a little about myself and how I run my practice.”

“Okay,” I said.

Dr. Lawson smiled, because this was the first response from me since we sat down. She nodded her head in agreement and began to speak about college life, how it was for her, and how she transitioned from college to the professional world. She intrigued me with the subtle conversation she was having, in essence with herself. I felt she knew I was listening to every word she spoke.

“Emily, let me ask you a few short and simple questions regarding your physical condition. We can take it from there, if that’s OK with you?” Dr. Lawson continued.

I gave her a quizzical look as to what it was she was rambling on about. She asked me a few non-invasive questions about headaches, body aches, tension in my muscles, blurred vision, etc. I was confused about this line of questioning until she wrapped things up at the end of our session. I can say now, Dr. Lawson was good. She definitely got my attention by talking about the one thing that weighed heavily on me—college life. I decided I wouldn’t fight the process anymore. I began to open up just a little and answer Dr. Lawson's questions. I started by describing my physical symptoms as well as my concerns. By the hour's end, I felt more at ease, and believed that the first session had gone smoothly. Dr. Lawson prescribed that I take an antidepressant. She advised that I take the medication for thirty days, and we scheduled weekly therapy sessions for the next sixty days.

I began to feel better after each visit and began having a better understanding of my emotions. In essence, I experienced multiple revelations. I still went through good days, bad days, happiness, turmoil and sadness—all feelings that were a result of the bad choices tied to my lifestyle and behavior, and my family issues. And how I dealt with truth, hurt and deceit.

My first revelation examined how I struggled with the illicit affair I had had with Jonathon Saxton, the older married man. I had fallen deeply in love with him. But I had disguised my feelings for fear of getting hurt. I had known that with everything that transpired in our relationship, I was wrong. I had been selfish and sought my own personal pleasure and self-gratification. As a result, I had aborted a precious life.

This realization occurred around the same time of a life- changing experience. While attending a computer engineering and graphic design seminar held annually in Los Angeles, California, I saw this handsome man walk across the room. I almost dropped a bottle of water because he resembled Jonathan, my high-school love. I hadn't seen him in almost six years. Not long after, as I was leaving the venue, by chance accident I ran into Jonathan. He was indeed the man I had seen earlier, and damn he was still fine as ever. I wasn't too bad myself, I must say. We greeted each other fondly, chatted for a bit, and then decided to go to a small café. Once there we talked for hours over coffee. We exchanged apologies and truths were exposed. We enjoyed each other's company, and agreed to get together again. Over the next few months, we continued to get together and got to know each other as older adults. It wasn't long before we began dating again. Unbelievably, our love had never dissipated, it was stronger than ever. We were married after a year, and immediately started a family. Today we have two beautiful children, Jonathan Jr. and Serenity. I chose Sarah to be the Godparent of our two babies, our precious gems.

As for Jonathan's children from his previous marriage, they are grown. Both are living their lives happily in Orlando, Florida. Jonathan's oldest child, Denise, is married and expecting her first child, and his son, Daniel, is a bachelor enjoying sunny Florida. I couldn't believe it—in three months we would be grandparents. I am just as excited as Jonathan to meet our first grandchild. Our relationships with the older kids are great. Things started off kinda rocky, but we overcame that obstacle, too.

Through several heartfelt talks, Jonathan over time had continued to disclose more about his life when he was married. I did not know that Jonathan, selfishly, had used me to escape the horror in which he was living. His wife of ten years was dying from ovarian cancer. And while she said she wanted to see him happy, she had asked that he respect her and their marriage and not bring another woman into their home. Still, she said she wanted him to find joy in his life. He told me she had been aware of me, but she never knew my age or that I was a former student.

Jonathan had not wanted to see her hurt and disappointed by his choice of dating a high-school girl. While we hadn't started dating until I had turned 18, most adults would still have considered me a child at that age. Jonathan confessed all of this to me. He even showed me a letter written by his wife that requested that he seek and find happiness—he said his wife had left the letter in her Bible. Jonathan held on to that Bible and the letter—they served as a constant reminder for how strong, beautiful and loving she was. I agreed he should. I could not deny him that comfort.

I thought to myself, the Bible appears to be a sacred place to hide letters, truths and lies. But who am I to judge? I use my Bible for prayer and private keepsakes.

My second revelation was addressing the devastation I felt in finding out the truth about daddy and Mrs. Hutchkins. I ached for mamma's heart. I was angry and wanted to hate daddy, but I couldn't. He was the best father anyone could ask for. I was confused as to why I, nor mamma or Aunt June could not maintain ill will or other bad feelings toward him. I concluded that it was all the love daddy showered us with while on Earth and God's powerful existence that showed us how to forgive, accept and move forward.

My third revelation came a number of years later. After, I was married I still would meet with Dr. Lawson. This revelation was that I struggled with my sexuality. I wasn't sure if I was a lesbian, bisexual or an experimentalist. I loved and fell in love with Sarah, but I loved Jonathan like no other. Sarah and I were the best of friends. My only fear was that we might have the urge to cheat on my loving husband, Jonathan. Dr. Lawson told me I needed to tell Jonathan the truth about Sarah. Eventually, I did just that. Jonathan had accepted Sarah into his life. She was the Godmother of our children. I assured Jonathan that I would never cheat on him. After that, Jonathan told me if I had the desire to be with Sarah, to be honest with him. Jonathan loved me that much.

Following my conversation with Jonathan, Dr. Lawson recommended a family therapist. Shortly thereafter, Jonathan, Sarah and I went to family therapy—together. Sarah confessed that she still lusted after me from time to time. Jonathan looked at her with a stare that I didn't quite understand. I had never before seen that look in his eyes. I asked Jonathan was he okay?

“Yes, I am,” Jonathan said, and continued in a low raspy voice, “I will be the only lover to Mrs. Emily Sims-Saxton, unless she decides otherwise.”

I snapped my neck and looked at Jonathan. I remarked, “Jonathan what are you saying?” I stared at him for a moment. I was able to read his mind and felt his thoughts pouring over me. I knew then Jonathan gave Sarah and me his blessing with transgression. Jonathan knew deep down in his soul, heart and spirit that things could change in an instance if I chose to live my life as a lesbian.

“If you feel the urge to have sexual intimacy with Sarah, you have to include me,” he replied. I believed that Jonathan felt if he gave me consent, then that would stop me from possibly sneaking around, committing adultery or jeopardizing our family bond. I tried to shake those rambling thoughts and at least give Jonathan a chance to explain, but I was still a skeptic and so was Sarah.

Sarah and I looked at each other in disbelief. The therapist spoke in a high-pitched tone, saying, “Although this is not considered normal behavior, there is nothing wrong with the three of you exploring your sexuality if each of you are in consent."

We all spoke in unison like robots, saying o-k-a-y.

The therapist again broke the mood and advised us to be careful that no one gets hurt. We agreed wholeheartedly that honesty and trust would be the premise of our relationship. Needless to say, we had a few ménage à trois. They were fun, explosive and exhilarating! Our sexual appetites were fully satisfied beyond this world. However, after Sarah met her "Mr. Right," and Jonathan and I had second thoughts, we collectively decided to end our sexual trysts.

It had felt great having both of my longtime lovers touching me at once. I had craved for them more than they would ever know. My sexual appetite was always fulfilled in true ecstasy and multiple orgasms during each encounter. I get out of breath every time I talk or think about it. However, I was somewhat happy to end our sexual trysts because I wanted Jonathan to penetrate me and me only. As it was, Sarah just wanted temporary penetration, a few hard strokes and she was okay.

Sarah loved to devour my love button with skillful strokes of her flickering tongue. I was honored that they both wanted me that bad but sharing them together began bothering me a little. But once the orgasms started again, all that shit went out the window and all I could think about was fucking until I couldn't breathe. One night after Sarah left, I told Jonathan that while I enjoyed them both wholeheartedly, I couldn't share him anymore. I wanted to always devour him with my mouth or my love spot—by myself. He was just that damn delicious and so damn fine. As we laid in bed and talked we both got horny and started making passionate love until the sun came up. That's when we knew it had to come to an end.

We met with Sarah the next morning for breakfast to talk it through with her. As we began to break the news of our changing feelings, Sarah stopped us and said, "I know you both all too well and I already picked up on some vibes that were a little off. At least until we all began having orgasms at once and the energy was elevated."

Sarah looked at me and said, softly, "Look Emily, I would never do anything to jeopardize our friendship and I will abide with the decision we conclude here." Sarah looked at me one last time and continued,

"Baby, your body is heavenly, and I enjoyed the feel and touch of your tenderness including the taste of your sweet juices. That's why I enjoyed our sexual trysts so much." Sarah turned to Jonathan and said, "Your penis is absolutely gorgeous, but I know you have reserved it for my girl here—although I enjoyed every stroke and penetration, it wasn't enough."

Sarah married Sampson Freeman, who she met two years earlier at a New Year's Eve party. It had been love at first sight. The energy between the two of them was magnetic, and almost mesmerizing. They married six months after their chance meeting and today they have a beautiful family. Our families are close, with an unbreakable bond. I am the Godmother to Sarah's three adorable children—Mattie, Sampson Jr. and Trinity. We didn't tell Sampson the truth about our sexual history. We decided that it was best we leave it that way. Instead, we lived our dreams and loved life as we had mapped it to be.

TEN: *CLOSURE*

I have matured, learned many life lessons and accepted responsibility for my actions. I've learned that life is a journey and will take you on two parallel roads called "The Life of Right" and "The Life of Wrong." It is up to you which direction you take and how you face any obstacles that arise. Staying true to yourself and believing in your morals is the sanctity of life with peace that beholds you.

I sit in my study and think back to my college years. I remember my home visits over holidays and the lengthy conversations I would have with mamma. Mamma would reveal certain things I never spoke of, but she knew about. The one thing she never knew, and I had hoped she would never find out, was the abortion. I remember vividly how mamma sat me down one night for one of our talks. It was cold outside, and mamma had a comfy fire burning. Mamma said, "Baby I know, see and hear everything." I thought to myself what would she see and hear if I did everything (all my dirt) outside of the home? Mamma looked deep into my eyes and said, "One day when you have a family, you will understand what I mean."

As the years passed and I grew from a young girl to womanhood and wife and motherhood, I came to understand what mamma was trying to tell me. See, it's not what you do, did or have done out of eyesight that tells a story. It is your everyday behavior—demeanor, subtle changes, mood swings. Your eyes, words spoken, and most of all, a mother's intuition, becomes meaningful. All these subtle giveaways can be called "body language." As an older woman, this is now clear to me, and I try to share this clarity with others. Parents pay close attention to your children because they are telling you everything—well, almost everything—without you even asking. Parents have the magical skill of figuring it out or putting together the pieces to the puzzle. I too have the gift of knowing my children, hell even my husband, better than they know themselves. Yes, a woman's instinct. Before you ask, I have finally figured out who I am, supposed to be, and want to be.

Sarah too has reached a blissful peace in her relationship with Sampson. Years after we ended our tryst, and after their marriage, she reluctantly told Sampson everything, even though she was full of fear of losing him. Sampson, however, told Sarah that his love for her ran deeper than any valley on earth. Today, happiness is their true meaning of life and love together.

Yes, my life, and my journey—it has been a voyage with many detours. How about yours? That "lost girl," I can't identify with anymore. I have found my true identity and purpose. I am living life as a free spirit and as a mother within the family structure, and I have my tribe with me every step of the way, as we trample this thing called "Life on Earth" in its truest form!

BOOK CLUB QUESTIONS

1. Is Emily really lost or is it her soul hasn't been fed?

2. Should Emily continue to call June "Aunt June" since they know they are sisters? Should they reveal this revelation to the family?

3. Did Emily's mother really know about the abortion?

4. Should Emily have continued her therapy sessions with Dr. Lawson?

5. Do you think Emily truly forgives Jonathan?

6. Will Emily and Jonathan bring someone else into their bedroom?

7. Does Jonathan truly trust Emily?

8. Do you think Emily's sexual interest in women, especially with Sarah will remain dormant or will they secretly start and illicit affair?

ABOUT THE AUTHOR

D. Caldwell is married with one daughter. She is a supporter of many family members and friends. She continues to mentor those who seek her charm, wittiness and direct manner to many over the years. She has many interests, with travel, fashion and writing being her three passions. Caldwell has always wanted to express herself through fashion, but until recently, she has found her creative niche in writing. She is an employee working a 9-5 job and is now enveloping herself into an entrepreneur with the drive from her daughter's creative spirit. She is now branching out and is expressing herself more through her style, which can be complex. She is like a chameleon and can blend in with any environment. She has a grand presence and a unique style of her own. This is expressed through her work and has been carried over into her poetry, and now her fiction with Lost Girl: Who Am I?

The End!

www.ingramcontent.com/pod-product-compliance
Lightning Source LLC
La Vergne TN
LVHW020656100826
845148LV00012B/2514

* 9 7 8 0 5 7 8 4 1 4 2 1 8 *